SECRET MISSION #5: MIRROR WORLD

BY GREG FARSHTEY

MAY 2013

SCHOLASTIC INC.

No part of this publication may be reproduced, stored in a retrieval system, or transmitted in any form or by any means, electronic, mechanical, photocopying, recording, or otherwise, without written permission of the publisher. For information regarding permission, write to Scholastic Inc., Attention: Permissions Department, 557 Broadway, New York, NY 10012.

ISBN 978-0-545-51271-8

LEGO and the LEGO logo are trademarks of the LEGO Group. © 2013 The LEGO Group. Produced by Scholastic Inc. under license from the LEGO Group.

Published by Scholastic Inc. SCHOLASTIC and associated logos are trademarks and/or registered trademarks of Scholastic Inc.

12 11 10 9 8 7 6 5 4 3 2 1   13 14 15 16 17/0

Printed in the U.S.A.   40

First printing, May 2013

Prologue

Another reality . . .

The red-armored robot leapt from the low rooftop, landing sprawled on the floor of the alleyway. He had heard the sound of metal cracking when he hit the pavement. If he was lucky, it was just some internal armor plating that had given way, and not the hydraulics he needed to keep going. It was too late to stop now.

He looked over his shoulder, back toward the roofs. There was no sign of his pursuers, but he knew they would not be far behind. Some said no one ever escaped from the Citadel; others that it happened all the time but the escapees didn't live to tell anyone about it.

That thought got him back up on his feet. A bribed guard had told him there was a hide-out somewhere near here, the first stop on a long road to the far northern part of the galaxy. There were plenty of stories about that region — they said that his kind would be welcome there, even admired. That was hard to believe, but not being hunted for a while would be a relief.

He ran. Sometimes, it seemed he had been running for his whole life. Was it his fault he believed the things he believed, and acted on them? No. This galaxy was a mess and that made it all the more important that he use his abilities.

So I don't act like everyone else does, he often said to himself. *Is that a crime?*

As a matter of fact, the answer was yes. That was how he had wound up in the Citadel, looking at a life sentence (the only kind ever handed down there). That was why he risked everything to escape, because the alternative was worse. And he already knew he was never going back there, not unless it was with a rocket to smash the place open and set everyone free.

Before he could do that, though, he had to get away. That wasn't going to be so easy to do, as four jolters had just appeared on sky cycles. Each one carried an electro-staff with enough voltage to temporarily shut down the system of any robot who wasn't protected by ion-insulation. Since that particular material, also called "I-I," was only found in the vaults of the Citadel and had long ago been banned for use in the manufacture of robots, the jolters pretty much had their own way.

Like everyone else, though, these Citadel guards/bounty hunters had a weakness. They were solidly built, but their sky cycles, not so much—and if you got the jolters on foot, you could outrun them.

The fugitive flew around a corner and then stopped, his back pressed against the brick wall. As soon as he spotted a jolter, he hurled a fireball at the sky cycle. It melted through the outer metal and took out the internal wiring, which wasn't protected by armor. It dropped like a stone, taking the jolter with it and hitting the ground with a very satisfying crash.

Time to run again. He took off down the alley, but just before he reached the far end, another jolter appeared, hovering on a cycle. He turned back, only to see another closing in on him. The third was in the air above the alley, cutting off that route of escape.

Nowhere to go but down, the fugitive thought, unleashing his flame power at the pavement. It melted like wax and he dropped down into the maintenance tunnels below the street.

By the time the jolters blasted a larger opening that would allow them to make it through with their cycles, their quarry was long gone. But they showed no anger or frustration at their failure. In fact, they smiled at one another as they headed back to the Citadel.

They had done exactly what they were supposed to do.

The fugitive robot spent the next three hours making his way through the underground network of tunnels—doubling back on himself, leaving false trails, and doing every other trick he could think of to keep the jolters off his trail. When he was finally convinced it was safe, he emerged through a robothole onto the street.

He had calculated his position correctly. He was just one block from the safe house. It was important not to run now, as he didn't want to draw the wrong kind of attention to himself. He forced himself to walk as if everything was fine and he was in no hurry.

Reaching the door, he knocked four times, as he had been told to do.

"Who's there at this hour?"

"A storm chaser," he answered, repeating the password he had been given.

The door opened. Bright light inside the house silhouetted the figure who welcomed him. The fugitive took a step forward and then stopped. A shaft of moonlight had suddenly struck the face of the safe house's lone occupant, revealing a figure out of a nightmare.

"Voltix!" said the fugitive in shock.

"Who else?" Voltix smiled and hurled a blast of electricity that knocked the fugitive flat on his back, his systems struggling to compensate for the massive charge. "There are no corrupt guards in the Citadel, runner . . . just foolish prisoners with too much hope and too little processing power. But don't worry, we'll smarten you up."

Voltix walked up to his captive and rested an armored boot on his power core. "After all, Furno, we have plenty of time for teaching—the rest of your life."

Furno—Hero, prisoner, fugitive, and now prisoner again—closed his eyes and wished he had never been created to live in such a galaxy as this.

Back in this reality . . .

"Oh no," said Bulk. "Not again!"

The powerful Hero was standing before a security checkpoint, deep in the heart of Hero Factory. The station was manned by his fellow Hero, Evo, who looked a little uncomfortable with his duties.

"This is the third time in the last fifteen minutes I've been scanned," Bulk grumbled. "What is it about me everyone finds so fascinating all of a sudden?"

"Sorry, Bulk, it's orders from the top," said Evo. "That first scan was to look for weapons you weren't registered to carry. The second one was to match your construction against the manufacture tag. This one is to make sure, well, that your mind isn't being controlled by anyone . . . or anything."

Bulk grimaced. He and Furno had just finished a mission that involved battling scores of robots who were being controlled by alien brains on top of their heads. Neither of them had ever fallen prey to the brains, so there was no reason for anyone to think they were being mind-controlled. This whole thing was starting to get on his nerves.

"The only brain is *in* my head." said Bulk, "not on top of it. Now get out of the way, I'm late for a briefing."

"Um, we're done anyway," said Evo. "You're definitely . . . you."

"No one else wants to be." Bulk chuckled as he went down the hallway.

Stormer had called this top-priority briefing just that morning. Along with Bulk, Furno and Breez were also present in the room. Stringer was busy being debriefed on his last mission.

"Okay, I'm here. We can get started," Bulk joked as he walked in.

Stormer didn't crack a smile. "Sit down. We have a lot to cover in a short time."

Hitting a button on the monitor, Stormer caused a chemical formula to appear on the main screen. The other three Heroes looked at it, trying to make some sense of what they were seeing. Breez was the first to do so, and a harsh gasp escaped her mouth.

"Is this . . . is this something we can handle?" she asked.

"We don't know," Stormer answered. "Zib has been running calculations for days, but there's no way to be sure until we try."

"Excuse me," Furno broke in. "Does someone want to explain what this is all about?"

"It's about power," said Stormer.

"Isn't everything?" Bulk said.

Stormer ignored him. "That chemical formula, if brought into existence, could provide Hero Factory with almost limitless power. We would be able to take a quantum leap forward technologically and be better able to defend the galaxy against threats. But . . ."

"But?" repeated Furno.

"The energy would be highly unstable. If we don't control it, it could do serious damage to Hero Factory, maybe even Makuhero City itself. That's why we've scheduled a test for tomorrow. If we can generate a small amount of energy safely, we can build up to full use of a larger-model generator."

"You want us as security for when you flip the switch, or acting as bait for some lunatic villain who might want the formula?" asked Bulk.

"Neither, really," said Stormer. Even in the dim lighting of the briefing room, his white armor gleamed. "If the generator runs wild, we have to shut it down. I'll need all three of you to help me do that."

"Right," said Bulk. "Sounds fun. I'm in."

Furno glanced at him. "You are?"

"Sure," said Bulk. "My life hasn't been in serious jeopardy in at least a day. I'm overdue."

Karter walked into the visiting area of the Hero Factory prison. His wrists and legs were shackled to prevent him from attempting escape. Although he was sharing a cell block with hardened criminals like Core Hunter and Speeda Demon, the Heroes were taking special precautions with him.

Not that he blamed them. There was a conspiracy brewing in the galaxy against Hero Factory, and Karter was right in the middle of it. He had been arrested weeks before for attempting to manufacture a solar weapon that would have given the conspirators the power to seize control over a massive number of inhabited worlds. The Heroes wanted to know who was behind it, but Karter wasn't talking.

So they tossed him in a cell, but because they were just and merciful types, they had to let him have visitors. Besides, they were monitoring his conversations, hoping to learn something. Maybe they didn't know he knew about that, but he did.

Since they're so eager to learn, I'll just teach them a lesson they'll never forget, he thought to himself.

His visitor was a thin, nervous-looking robot named Perjast. They had met a long time ago when Karter was on another job, this time one that Hero Factory would have approved of. He was cleaning up an extremely corrupt planetary government with the help of Perjast, a low-level official more scared of Karter than of his bosses. Over the years since, Perjast had done little jobs for Karter, and in return, Karter hadn't let the robot informer's ex-employers know who had helped put them in jail.

"Did you do what I said?" asked Karter.

Perjast nodded.

Karter relaxed just a little bit. He'd had some of his old friends on the outside provide Perjast with a scrambler unit that could slip past most scans. When activated, it would alter the words spoken in a room so that any monitors would pick up a perfectly innocent conversation. Only the people speaking would hear what was really being said.

"What about the rest?" asked Karter, now confident he could talk without being overheard.

Perjast shrugged. "I guess."

"What do you mean, you guess?" demanded Karter. "Did you get it or didn't you?"

"When they wired in the scrambler, they put some other equipment in, too," answered Perjast. "I don't know what it was, and they said I was better off not knowing. Listen, how much trouble am I in just for coming here? I don't need Hero Factory on my back."

Karter wasn't listening. How had his employers figured on getting him the device he needed if Perjast didn't even know he had it? And what else could they have supplied him with when they were giving him the scrambler? What was this all about?

Part of the answer came in the next instant. Perjast stood up, a little unsteady, and then promptly pitched forward, his systems shutting down. Karter could see he was still functioning, but only at a low level. Something was seriously wrong.

At least, it was for Perjast—Karter, on the other hand, had just figured the whole thing out and was a very satisfied robot.

The whole plan hinged on one simple fact: For a professional like Karter, breaking out of a Hero Factory cell was not that difficult. What was much harder, almost impossible these days, was getting out of Hero Factory itself. Security was much tighter ever since the mass breakout of months before. Still, all he needed was a few minutes of freedom to pull off what he had in mind.

It started in the repair bay. Perjast had been taken there after his mysterious shutdown, and Karter snuck there from his cell without being detected. As Karter expected, it was just a temporary condition and the robot was already powering up again, if slowly. Fortunately, his inner workings were still exposed as the Hero Factory technicians tried to figure out what made him collapse in the first place.

Karter snuck through the bay until he got close to Perjast. Yes, there it was, hidden behind some of the fallen robot's circuitry: a solid-light hologram generator. That was the piece of equipment Karter needed to destroy Hero Factory.

Swiftly and surely, without doing any damage to Perjast, he extracted the item. It was fortunate that none of the Hero Factory techs had noticed and removed it. With his prize in hand, Karter slipped back to his cell.

He had conceived his strategy when he learned about Stormer's plan to test a new energy source. Although that was top secret, Hero Factory had to let the governments of neighboring worlds know about it, just in case something went wrong. Karter's employers had spies on those worlds and they had fed the information to him.

This news made it all so simple. To wreck Hero Factory, simply sabotage the test. But the testing chamber was high security — heat sensors, weight sensors, three-foot-thick walls — no one was walking in or out of there without setting off a dozen alarms. *No one real, that is,* thought Karter.

Back in his cell, Karter waited until the guards were at the other end of the corridor. Then he triggered the solid-light hologram generator. What materialized in his cell looked like a robot made all of smooth silver, with no facial features or other distinguishing features. It was blank, in more ways than one: simply waiting for its creator to give orders.

Karter did just that. "Break into the Hero Factory testing center, rearrange the beta and zed circuits, and make certain not to leave a trace of what you did," he said. "Then cease to exist."

The hologram walked through the wall and was gone.

Using normal holograms for sabotage had never been practical in the past. Images made of light could be detected by the heat they gave off, plus they were unable to hold any physical objects. They made good decoys, since they looked real, but that was about it.

Solid-light holograms were another matter entirely. They had enough mass to be able to hold a tool or a weapon, but not so much that they set off alarms. They gave off no heat. For very brief periods, they were even able to bend light around them, making themselves invisible. The technology was incredibly expensive and even outlawed on some worlds, but very little was beyond Karter's employers.

Of course, there was a negative side to this plan. If Hero Factory was vaporized, Karter would be, too. He was counting on there being enough time for Stormer to issue an evacuation order. Karter would find a way to make sure he was the first one out.

He lay down on his cot and imagined the hologram easily penetrating the testing chamber, altering circuits to ensure there would be a disaster so terrible no one would want a Hero Factory facility in their sector ever again. Even if some, or most, Heroes survived this, their organization would be shattered forever.

Mission accomplished, he thought with a smile.

The next day, Stormer, Bulk, Furno, and Breez reported to the testing chamber. All security monitors showed no intrusions during the night. All lights on the new generator were green. No one in the room could know that a hologram capable of altering key circuits could also sabotage the monitoring board to make it look like everything was just fine.

"Is everyone ready?" asked Stormer.

"Yes," said Furno.

"Do it," said Bulk.

"Yes, okay, go ahead," said Breez. She looked around nervously. Something about this place didn't *feel* right, but she couldn't see anything wrong. She wasn't going to waste Stormer's time by voicing what nothing but instinct was telling her.

Stormer hit a series of buttons and pushed a red lever up to its maximum setting. There was a loud hum as the generator came to life. The four Heroes waited expectantly. If the process was working correctly, the hum would quiet down and neon green energy would begin flowing through the transparent tubing that led to the power cells in the walls.

The hope for a smooth test died in 1.6 seconds.

Instead of growing softer, the hum got louder. Blinding light shot out from every seam in the generator. All four robots felt a vibration in their systems — something unfamiliar and horribly wrong — which told them everything they needed to know about what would happen next.

"Shut it down!" yelled Bulk. "It's on overload!"

Stormer glanced at the monitor screen. All the lights were still green. "We've been sabotaged!" he said. "It's out of control!"

Furno worked the main control panel

furiously, trying to put energy dampers into place to prevent disaster. The panel resisted every attempt he made, until he slammed his metal fist into it in frustration.

"We're locked out!" he shouted. "I can't stop it!"

Stormer punched an alarm button on the wall. A loud siren sounded all over Hero Factory. "This is Stormer! Evacuation order 1-A. Repeat, evacuation order 1-A."

"That sounds like a good idea," said Bulk. "Let's go."

"We can't," Stormer answered. "We have to stay here."

"Why?" asked Breez. "We still have time to make it out of Hero Factory."

Stormer shook his head. "If we open the chamber, the energy will flood the facility in seconds. We don't know what it might do—it could be lethal to all robotic life at this level. The chamber has to stay sealed to contain as much as we can. I'm . . . sorry."

With any other group of robots, there might

have been arguments, even physical fights, at this news. But these were Heroes. They understood what that label meant — sometimes, a Hero had to sacrifice himself or herself for the good of others. So where there might have been anger, there was just acceptance.

They didn't have long to wait. There was an intense flare of energy that melted the walls of the generator, light and heat washing over them in what they felt certain were the final seconds of their existence.

And then, there was only darkness. . . .

2

Stormer had seen and done a lot of things in his life. He had been places most other beings could only dream of, fought monsters and power-mad villains, and seen the best and worst that robots were capable of. It was very hard to surprise him.

But even he had to admit being shocked to discover he was still alive.

He sat up, his mind already assessing the situation at lightning speed. Nearby, Bulk, Furno, and Breez were just reviving. Stormer's internal systems check revealed no serious damage, meaning the generator overload had not been as dangerous as it seemed at first. That was the good news.

The bad news was that the four of them were no longer in Hero Factory, or anywhere that Stormer recognized. He stood up and looked around. They appeared to be in a warehouse, dusty and long disused. A quick sensor scan of the general area revealed that it was mostly abandoned buildings, most on the verge of falling down.

"You take us to the nicest places," Bulk said, smiling. "But at least we're all in one piece."

"Spatial displacement," said Breez, running her hand along the wooden walls of the warehouse.

"Spatial what?" said Furno.

"We've been moved through space," Breez explained. "The energy from the generator must have done it. We're on some other world in some other part of the galaxy."

"Well, that's a relief," said Furno. "All we have to do is get a ship and we can head back to Hero Factory, then."

Stormer led the team out of the warehouse. Outside, the streets were dark and deserted.

Wherever they were, no one cared much about this neighborhood.

The still air was suddenly ripped open by a scream. It came from down the block. All four Heroes ran toward the sound. When they got there, they saw one robot being attacked by another. The attacker was trying to steal a box of tools from his victim.

The Heroes charged. Breez and Furno crashed into the attacking robot, slamming him against a wall. Stormer and Bulk helped his victim back to his feet. The rescued robot looked at them, puzzled.

"Well?" he said after a moment, offering the box to them. "Take it! What are you waiting for?"

"We don't want your tools, sir," said Stormer. "We saw you were in trouble and came to help. Are you all right?"

The robot looked stunned. He glanced over at the captured thief. "You don't want . . . ? Oh no . . ." Then, before anyone could stop him, he ran off into the night, shouting, "Lawbreakers! Lawbreakers!"

The thief sneered at Furno, saying, "He's

right. But you won't get far. They know how to deal with the likes of you in this city."

"You're the one who's going to jail, pal," said Furno.

"What for?" asked the thief. "I haven't done a thing wrong."

"Tie him up," said Stormer. "We'll tell the first law officer we meet where to find him. For now, we need to figure out where we are."

"You don't know what planet you're on?" The thief laughed. "So you're lawbreakers *and* aliens, then?"

"Hey, Stormer," said Bulk. "Let's find a rooftop. Something's really not right here."

Leaving the bound thief in an alley, Stormer and his team headed for a warehouse roof. Once there, Bulk pointed up at the stars. "What do you see?" he asked.

Stormer and the others looked up at the night sky. After a few moments, Stormer said, "That makes no sense."

"What are you talking about?" asked Breez. "It's just the sky and the stars."

"No, I get it," said Furno. "Look at the constellations, Breez."

She did. "Yes, I see them, so what . . . wait a minute. I recognize that one . . . and that one . . . but that can't be."

"But it is," said Bulk. "Those are the same constellations we see every night above Hero Factory. We're in Makuhero City, folks . . . We didn't leave our planet . . . we're home."

Sensor scans confirmed Bulk's statement. The team was at the same coordinates they had been when the generator overloaded. Only now, those coordinates weren't in Hero Factory, but a rundown warehouse district.

"Theories?" said Stormer.

"It's all a bad dream," said Bulk. "Hey, it's as good a theory as any."

"Maybe we weren't moved in space, but in time?" offered Breez. "Maybe this is the city in the past, or the future."

"It's not the past," said Furno. "I studied the history of Makuhero City. It never looked like this."

Stormer had to agree. Mr. Makuro had created a place other planets aspired to imitate. It had never suffered the sort of neglect obvious here. "The future, then?" he wondered out loud. "But I would have expected the robots to be more advanced . . . the two we encountered looked the same as any other we might have met yesterday."

"I have another question," said Bulk. "How come the robot we rescued thought we were crooks, too? And when he found out we weren't . . . that's when he panicked."

"We're not going to find any answers up here," Stormer replied. "Let's scout around."

The most familiar landmarks for any Hero in Makuhero City were, of course, the Assembly Tower and the other structures that made up Hero Factory. Yet there was no sign of these anywhere. And it didn't seem as if they had been there and were torn down — the buildings standing in their place had construction dates stamped on them that went back years before Hero Factory had come into being. They had always been there . . . and evidently Hero Factory never had.

"I don't understand," said Breez. "How could Hero Factory have not been here? What power could just . . . erase it?"

"I'm not sure," said Stormer, "but I think I'm getting an idea. And there's one place in Makuhero City still standing—that's where we need to go for answers."

He didn't have to tell the others what he was talking about, for they could all see the familiar outline of Makuhero University against the night sky.

"Von Nebula University?!" exclaimed Furno. "Is this someone's idea of a joke?"

The Heroes were staring up at the main administration building of the university they knew so well. It looked almost exactly the same as they remembered, with one exception: the name carved in stone above the doors.

"If this is some kind of a test, we can stop now," said Breez. "Furno and I aren't rookies anymore, but, fine—you want me to say this is giving me the creeps? It is."

"This isn't any test," said Bulk. "Or, if it is, we're all in it with you."

"Let's go," Stormer said, starting up the steps.

"Wait a second!" said Bulk. "You're just going to walk right into a place named after your worst enemy?"

"If I'm right, it won't matter," said Stormer.

The four Heroes went in through the two heavy front doors. Inside, the air was cool and the place was quiet. Padding on the floors even muffled the sounds of the robots' metal feet. A thin, small robot sat behind a curved wooden desk.

"May I help you?" she asked.

"We're looking for some information on local history," said Stormer.

"It's for our homework," Bulk added with a smile.

"You seem a little old to be students," the clerk replied.

"Robots going back to school," countered Bulk. "It's a big thing right now."

"Well, you can check the east wing. That's where the Histotron is—do you know how to operate it?"

"I'll figure it out," said Stormer. The last thing he wanted was anyone coming along and seeing exactly what it was they were researching. "Thank you."

Furno had heard about the Histotron but never used it. It was a machine that downloaded data on historical events right into your computer brain. Using it saved an enormous amount of time, although trying to learn too much too fast could cause damage to internal processors.

It was a surprisingly large machine with what looked to Furno to be a crude headset design. Breez confirmed this, saying, "I've seen pictures of this machine—it didn't look like that."

"I'm not surprised," said Stormer. "I don't think this is precisely the same machine. But hopefully its function is similar."

Stormer sat down and fitted the headset on his head. "All I have to do is focus on what I want to learn about and the machine does the rest. Furno, turn it on."

Furno flipped the main switch. Instantly, Stormer screamed in agony. Furno immediately shut it down while Bulk rushed to free the Alpha Team leader from the headset.

"I knew something wasn't right about this thing," said Bulk. "Who trusts a machine in Von Nebula University?"

"No, no," Stormer said, leaning on his friend for support. "I saw it all. I got my answers."

"But you weren't even connected for more than a few seconds," said Breez.

"A few seconds for you, a thousand years for me," Stormer answered. "That machine works fast. We have to get out of here—we have a lot to talk about, Heroes."

Outside, Stormer led them to an alleyway.

Once he was sure no one else was around, he said, "The constellations are correct—this is Makuhero City, although now it's called Von Nebula City. The reason we see no signs of Hero Factory is that it never existed."

"Never existed . . . ?" said Breez. "How—?"

"You asked what power could just erase it from existence," Stormer said to her. "Right then, I saw the answer. The only power that could do that is the one we were testing just hours ago."

"You mean the overload changed history somehow?" asked Furno.

Stormer shook his head. "Worse than that, in some ways. Team, I don't believe this is our universe. I think the accident in the test lab threw us into a parallel dimension where *there is no Hero Factory*. And unless we can find some way home, we're going to be trapped here for the rest of our lives."

Back in the university library, the clerk examined the Histotron. Its memory banks retained a record of any search done in the last thirty days, including keywords. She scanned the list of terms searched for by Stormer, and frowned. Hero Factory? Makuhero City? None of these made any sense, and she knew what she had to do under the circumstances.

She went back to her desk and switched on the communication system. "Citadel? This is L-22 at VNU Sector 1, access code 350XY72G. Please respond."

A harsh, mechanical voice replied, "Access code confirmed. Please state the nature of your emergency."

L-22 gave a detailed account of all that had happened. "Since they were looking for a place called 'Hero Factory,' I naturally thought the Citadel should be informed," she finished.

There was a soft whirring sound as the robot on the other end processed what she had said. Then it responded, "Your report has been noted and logged. If further action is determined to be warranted, the Citadel will respond appropriately. However . . ."

"Yes?"

"This incident does not rise to the level of an emergency under Citadel Code 14-B. You have therefore misused the emergency line, L-22."

"What? No!" the clerk cried. "Who knows who they could be? What if they're spies, or even . . ." Her voice dropped to a whisper. "Heroes?"

"Citadel judgment is final. You have misused the emergency line. Please report immediately to a destruction booth, L-22. Your replacement, L-23, has already been dispatched to your location. End transmission."

L-22 stared at the communicator for a moment. Then she neatly packed her personal belongings into a box and checked her computer station to make sure it was ready for her successor.

Satisfied that everything was in order, she departed the university, heading for the local destruction booth. The only thought she could console herself with was that those four strangers would probably be joining her there soon.

Speeda Demon hated working behind a desk. As he often said, "Speed—it's part of my name—and I can't race when I'm sitting still!" But when Von Nebula said you worked the consoles, you did it, because the alternative was getting tossed into a robot-made black hole.

Of course, the punishment didn't really fit the crime. Speeda Demon had robbed the same bank twice in two months. Last week, he passed it by, out of sheer boredom, and hit a gem convoy instead. Passing up an opportunity to commit theft was technically against the law, but being a high-ranking member of the Citadel, Speeda Demon figured he could get away with it.

He should have known better. Splitface had been in the neighborhood and saw the whole thing, and being the ambitious little sneak that he was, had immediately notified the Citadel. Speeda Demon could have been exiled to the frontier or even vaporized, but Von Nebula decided that making him stay in one place for a week would be torture enough.

That's why he was manning the central communications console when L-22's message was sent upstairs. At first, he just did a quick scan, as he did with most of the other static passed along by the robot operators. Then something caught his eye and he went back and took a second look.

Something was nagging him. He leaned back in his chair and struggled to retrieve a memory. He used to have a really good long-term memory, until he tangled with Core Hunter over a haul of precious metals and lost. The resulting energy drain messed up some of his memory circuits and he never got around to getting them repaired.

Still, he should have been able to remember a name as unique as . . .

"Hero Factory."

Speeda Demon closed his eyes. Who was it that had said those words to him, and when? What had been going on at the time that made them stick in his head?

Then he recalled a face he had not seen in many years, that of Akiyama Makuro. An ultra-rich industrialist and inventor, some people said that the only thing Makuro didn't own was space itself, and that was only because there was no one to buy it from. He had pioneered stunning advances in robotics, mechanized manufacturing, and power core design, and made trillions of credits doing it. But even really, really smart robots can do things that are stupid.

In Makuro's case, that was reactivating one morning and deciding he had to use his wealth to accomplish something more than just expanding his businesses. He wanted to do "good" — this despite the fact that the natural order of things in the universe was that nice robots finished last. Since the days when the first crude factory robot sabotaged another in order to get a better position on the assembly line, it had been a hard world. You were either a taker, or else someone who got taken.

Makuro was determined to change all that, a little at a time. He converted one of his larger factories from making aerocar assembly robots to making "Heroes." They were programmed to be noble, self-sacrificing, and good. Speeda Demon was surprised that he could still remember their names: Stormer, Furno, Thresher, Bulk, Stringer, and of course, Von Ness.

He remembered when the news first spread that Makuro was pursuing this insane idea. Most robots laughed about it—imagine, trying to sic "Heroes" on this galaxy! That was like tossing mice into a wild rhalos pen—fun for the wolf-lizard, not so much for the mice.

The laughter stopped when the "Heroes" started making pests of themselves. They were actually interfering with robberies, stopping acts of sabotage and industrial spying, and they even prevented Toxic Reapa from blackmailing an entire city by threatening to turn its bay into poisonous sludge. Makuro's wild idea was starting to prove inconvenient for a lot of powerful robots.

Something had to be done.

Fortunately, not all of Makuro's robots were as pure as he would have liked. Von Ness had decided pretty quickly that fighting an entire galaxy was no way to live, and he would rather be on the winning side of the battle to come. He sold the plans for Makuro's factory to a professional thief named Black Phantom, who put together a team to bring the place down.

It worked. The factory was wrecked, the Heroes battered and scattered, and as for Makuro . . . well, Speeda Demon had been telling the story for years that he had deactivated the industrialist. Whether it was true or not didn't matter, since one way or the other, no one had seen Makuro since that day. Meanwhile, Von Ness changed his name to Von Nebula and started taking over the gangs.

But the really important thing was something Makuro had told Von Ness, and Von Ness had told Speeda Demon later on—that if Makuro's venture had been successful, he was planning to name the site "Hero Factory."

Why would anyone be looking that term up after all these years? wondered Speeda Demon. *Who else would even know about it?*

He saw no other choice. Much as he hated going upstairs to see the boss, he was going to have to bring this news to Von Nebula. If he was lucky, maybe it would get him off desk work.

Oh, who am I kidding? Speeda Demon said to himself as he headed for the turbo elevator. *I'll be lucky if I just survive the meeting.*

Von Nebula was sitting in the shadows when the private elevator opened to disgorge Speeda Demon. The undisputed leader of this sector of space did not even bother to look up. All of his visitors knew the simple equation—either the message was urgent, or the messenger was rapidly extinct.

"Um, Von Nebula, sir . . ." Speeda Demon began. "I . . . there's something I thought . . . someone is asking about Hero Factory."

Von Nebula stirred at the sound of the name, but so slightly that it was imperceptible to his subordinate. His voice, when he spoke, sounded close by and far away at the same time. "Go on."

Speeda Demon related the whole story as quickly as he could. When he was done, there was a long silence. Then Von Nebula rose from his chair. Speeda Demon immediately averted his eyes, as that was never a pleasant sight.

"Bring the clerk here," said Von Nebula.

"L-22? Well, I think she was sent to a destruction booth, actually. Something about misusing the emergency system . . ."

"Find her," Von Nebula said, his words wrapping around Speeda Demon like a venomous snake. "If she has been exterminated, you will be joining her."

Speeda Demon's cycle was waiting for him when he hit the ground floor of the Citadel. Its nav computer had already calculated the location of the destruction chamber nearest to Von Nebula University. Assuming L-22 was a properly frightened citizen, she would go there, as opposed to taking a long last walk around the city before reporting for obliteration.

Traffic wasn't a problem. Even though he was pretty low level, he was still considered Citadel inner circle. That meant he had authorization to run over anyone who was in his way, and everyone knew it. At the distinctive sound of his motorcycle, pedestrians dove for cover and other motorists veered onto the sidewalk.

There was a long line at D.B. #27. L-22 was still about sixteen robots away from the booth. Speeda Demon skidded to a stop beside her. "Get on," he ordered.

"What?" L-22 answered, shocked. "I'm doing what I was told! I didn't do anything wrong!"

Speeda Demon sighed. Sometimes, the grip of fear the Citadel held everyone in wasn't such a good thing. Now and then, bored jolters would try to convince a condemned robot that they had been spared to get them to leave the line. Naturally, leaving the line topped the list of major offenses, and the punishment was . . . well, worse than staying in it. It was all in good fun, but it sometimes made legitimately pardoned offenders reluctant to accept their good fortune.

"I said, get on!" snarled Speeda Demon, grabbing L-22 and hauling her onto the back of his cycle. Before she could protest, he had roared out into the street.

"Where are you taking me?"

Speeda Demon gave the question some thought before he answered, "Probably the last place you'd want to go."

There was a time when Von Nebula had almost everything he could want. He had successfully betrayed his fellow "Heroes" to the Legion of Darkness. With the do-gooders out of the way, he embraced the culture of the galaxy—one that promoted greed, larceny, deceit, and dishonor. From one neighborhood, he expanded his empire to include all of the city, and then the entire region of space. Even those planets he did not control knew enough not to cross him.

But somewhere along the way, Von Nebula decided it wasn't enough. His primary source of power was a Black Hole Orb Staff, which allowed him to create areas in space with such powerful gravity that not even light could escape from within them. *What would happen*, he often wondered, *if someone got my staff away from me? My vast holdings would disappear and I would have no way to retake them.*

Von Nebula could not accept that possibility. There had to be a way to safeguard his weapon so that no one could ever seize control of it.

In the end, he had found the perfect solution . . . or so it seemed.

Now I sit in the center of galactic power, he thought. *When I was a Hero, I had to keep my true self hidden away. I couldn't let Stormer and the others know where my true loyalties lay. And here I am, all these years later, still forced to conceal myself in the shadows. Does nothing ever change?*

He was distracted from his dark musings by the sound of his private elevator opening. L-22 stumbled into the cavernous room. Von Nebula could practically smell her fear.

"The robots who visited you tonight," he said. "Describe them. Leave no detail out."

Stammering, L-22 did her best to paint a word picture of the four robots that had come to the university. Now and then, Von Nebula would interrupt with a question. After a few minutes, she had run out of things to say and stood silent, waiting for a reaction.

"Is there nothing else?" asked Von Nebula. "Any fact, no matter how small, will be of benefit to the Citadel."

"Yes, there is something," she said, suddenly remembering. "When I checked the Histotron to see what they had searched for, the name of the robot who last used the machine was listed on the screen."

"And what was his name?"

"Stormer. Preston Stormer."

Von Nebula shot to his feet, so quickly that he stumbled forward into the light. L-22 found she could not stifle a scream.

She had heard the rumors, of course — everyone had — that Von Nebula had tried to incorporate the power of his staff into his robot body, only to have something go terribly wrong. But she had never imagined . . .

"That . . . cannot . . . be!" Von Nebula said, his words flying like laser bolts. "You are lying!"

"No, no, Your Highness!" L-22 insisted. "You can check for yourself! It's on the data recording."

Von Nebula took a step back into the darkness and struggled to calm himself. *Stormer? No, it was impossible. Not a second time. I had seen to that, surely.*

"If . . . if you are telling the truth, you will find a job waiting for you in the Citadel," he said finally. "If not, you will disappear and no one will ever find you. Do you understand?"

L-22 nodded. Then her mouth opened and a question came out, all on its own, despite her best efforts to stop it. "Your Highness . . . what . . . what happened?"

She could see his eyes gleaming in the shadows. He gave the slightest of shrugs as he settled back into his chair, safely nestled in the dark.

"Stormer happened, my dear."

4

The four Heroes stood in an alleyway, their eyes fixed on the ominous shape of the Citadel silhouetted against the night sky. Jolters buzzed around the top of the huge fortress like moths around a particularly attractive flame.

"We have to get in there?" said Bulk in disbelief. "Gee, why not have us do something hard, like push the moon out of orbit?"

"I hate to say it, but he's right," said Furno. "We've cracked our share of hideouts, but that place could hold an army—or hold one off."

"Of course he's right," said Stormer. "That's why we aren't going to break in. We're going to get an invitation to visit."

The Heroes slipped away. Breez had found an abandoned building not far from the Citadel, which Stormer and crew were now using as a base. They took seats around a battered old table.

"You're going to get us arrested, aren't you?" said Bulk. "Sure, we go out, save some lives, break up some thefts, and—wham!—they toss us in the Citadel for life. That's how we get inside, right?"

"Wrong," Stormer replied. "We can't take the chance that the cells are escape-proof. We don't know if there's tech here somewhere beyond what we can handle."

"That doesn't leave us very many options," said Breez. "If we're right, the only possible place we might find enough power to send us home is inside that building."

Stormer leaned back in his chair. "Breez, what's the first rule of battle on an alien world?"

"Make use of what you have around you," she replied instantly. "Use your environment."

"Right, and that's just what we're going to do."

"Well, from what you've told us," Bulk said,

"we're surrounded by crooks. This whole society rewards what we'd call 'crime' back home, and punishes anyone who tries to stop an 'honest thief' from 'earning' a living."

Stormer nodded. "Exactly. This society respects lawlessness, force, and power — especially power. Based on what I 'saw' in the Histotron, status is based on how many gangs you control, how much territory you have, how many robots answer to you. If we want to get into the Citadel, we need to make them think they have no choice about the invitation — that they *have* to deal with us.

"And this is how we're going to do it . . ." he began with a smile.

The next night saw a packed house at Von Nebula Stadium. The big event was a championship obstacle course race featuring robot runners from all over the galaxy. There were so many entrants that the promoters had created two separate courses and divided up the racers between them. They then sold a split ticket that allowed fans to cross back and forth between races and see both if they wished.

Outside the stadium, Splitface smiled. The gate receipts of a split ticket event were just perfect for him. Other thieves would certainly know that, too, and would most likely stay away tonight. He would have a clear field.

He couldn't help but get a laugh out of the sheer number of robots who turned out for things like this. Anyone with a decent computer in their head knew these races were fixed. The fun, he supposed, was trying to guess which runners had been paid to lose.

Splitface waited until the ticket seller had collected all the credits and sealed them inside a secure pouch. Then he signaled his gang to move in.

The robbery went off smoothly. They had the pouch in a matter of seconds, and it took only a little longer than that to persuade the ticket seller to give over the security code. Now all that was left was the getaway, but that could be done at leisure. It wasn't like anyone would be trying to stop them.

Splitface and his crew turned away from the stadium and headed for their jet cycles, all of which were parked side by side across the street. To their surprise, there was a robot in white armor standing by the cycles, admiring them.

"Hey!" said Splitface. "You want to get away from those?"

Stormer turned to look at the approaching gang. "Oh, I'm sorry. You need these to get away with the money, don't you?" He idly kicked one at the end of the row, which toppled over, taking all the others with it in a domino effect. "Oops."

"Comedians. I hate comedians," Splitface growled. "Unless they're dead ones, of course."

"Bet you'll get a laugh out of this, though," said Bulk. He was standing on a nearby rooftop. "Hand over the credits, Splitface. You're being robbed."

"What?" bellowed Splitface. "Who do you guys think you are? My crew will—"

"You mean this crew?" asked Furno.

Splitface turned to see his gang on the ground, with Furno and Breez standing over them.

"Are these the best this city has to offer?" said Breez. "If they are, we're going to take over this place by morning."

"You losers don't know who you're messing with," growled Splitface. "I've got friends at the Citadel."

"Good," said Stormer as he relieved Splitface of the security pouch. "Tell them Alpha Team says hello."

With that, the four robots disappeared into the night, leaving behind a very angry Splitface.

Jawblade loved pleasure cruises. They were just about his favorite thing in the world.

Not that he ever went on one—certainly nobody would ever invite him, plus he got land-sick when he was out of the water. But these cruises usually had rich robots on them with lots of jewels and precious metals. All he had to do was take a bite out of their boat and then offer to do the same to them unless they handed everything over.

He was so focused on his target that he never noticed the boat coming up behind him. It was only when the suction-cup-tipped arrow struck him and sent a jolt of electricity through his robot frame that he realized he wasn't alone.

"That hurt!" Jawblade roared. "Who the — ?"

"Hi there," said Stormer, standing at the wheel of the speedboat he and his team had borrowed. "I'm guessing you were planning to rob that ship?"

"Yeah, what's it to you?" said Jawblade. "It's a water robbery. That's what I do."

"Not today," said Furno. "See, we already robbed it."

Stormer suppressed a smile. Of course they hadn't actually committed a theft, but Furno seemed to be enjoying the role of bad guy.

"You already — what!?" said Jawblade. "I had

a Citadel okay for this job! You can't just muscle in and do someone else's robbery."

That was when Jawblade noticed that there was a fine metal wire attached to the arrow that was still stuck to him. An instant later, Bulk was yanking hard on the line, hauling Jawblade up and out of the water.

"We just did," said Stormer. "From now on, you want to pull a job, you get permission from *us*. If you ask politely, we might even say yes."

"Are you crazy? Do you know what Von Nebula would do to me if I did that? Do you know what he's going to do to you?"

"Von Nebula?" said Furno. "Oh, right, he's the robot with that tired old gravity gag. They laugh at stuff like that where we come from."

Stormer reached out and clamped Jawblade's mouth shut. "You tell Von Nebula that there's no room in this part of space for amateurs. Alpha Team is taking over. Tell him maybe there's a place for him in our organization, if he plays things smart."

Jawblade tried to say something. Stormer

shrugged and let him open his mouth.

"You think Von Nebula's going to work with you?"

"Who said anything about *with* us?" Stormer replied. "He can work *for* us."

The reports started trickling into the Citadel the next day. By the day after, the trickle had become a flood. All of the messages said the same thing: Some new outfit calling itself Alpha Team was cutting in on Citadel business and getting away with it.

The descriptions of this daring gang matched the ones given by L-22. That was good news for her, but it posed a mystery for Von Nebula. Just who were these robots, and where had they come from?

One thing he knew for certain — this was not the Preston Stormer he had served with under Makuro all those years ago. After the Legion of Darkness attack, Stormer had vanished. Von

Nebula had figured he was gone for good and never gave him a second thought. That was a mistake. . . .

Somehow, Stormer had gotten wind that Von Nebula was going to try to absorb the power of the Orb Staff into himself. Right in the middle of the process, Stormer appeared, trying to stop him. There was a fight, some explosions, and damaged machinery running out of control, and, well. . . there was a reason Von Nebula had banned mirrors from the Citadel.

Stormer had not walked away from this action unharmed. No, Von Nebula made sure his old foe would carry a reminder of his deeds for all time. No technician, no repair bay, would ever be able to change that. Yet the description of the white-armored robot in charge of Alpha Team did come close to matching that of his hated enemy. And there was one thing more. . . .

The group of Heroes led by Stormer, before the Legion of Darkness smashed them all, was called Alpha Team.

Von Nebula considered what to do. He could

send Voltix and his jolters out to round up these intruders, but full-scale combat in Von Nebula City would be bad for business. Plus, the jolters were known for their "enthusiasm" and might destroy the enemy, leaving the Citadel with no more answers about their origins than before.

No, this called for diplomacy. Von Nebula's finger stabbed down on his control panel, hitting the red button that summoned XT4.

Of all the members of the Citadel's inner circle, XT4 was the only one Von Nebula had personally brought into being. After Makuro's disappearance, Von Nebula had seized all of the industrialist's properties. Among them was a plant that made robots for use in factories and manufacturing centers. Purely for his amusement, Von Nebula tried reprogramming one, which resulted in the creation of perhaps the most ruthless operative in the Citadel.

As the multi-armed robot entered Von Nebula's chambers, he bowed his head slightly in subservience. XT4's loyalty was unquestionable, as were his cold, businesslike approach to his job and complete lack of emotion. This made him a perfect go-between with Alpha Team. He would not succumb to anger, fear, or any attempt at bribery.

Von Nebula gave XT4 his instructions. He was to commit a brazen theft in the center of Von Nebula City, one that was sure to attract the attention of Alpha Team. From there, the rest would be simple.

XT4 departed on his mission. There was one other thing Von Nebula liked about his creation: XT4 was the only one who could look at his employer in the light of day without screaming.

XT4's computer mind rapidly calculated the action most likely to bring Alpha Team to him. A new shipment of protean space gems had recently been received from a frontier world, a payment for protection to Von Nebula. In return for this tribute, the Citadel would discourage its space-faring thieves from targeting that world.

If Alpha Team knew about the shipment, they would most likely try to steal it. If not, its sheer value would make any attempted theft one that would interest them.

Having downloaded all the details of the gems' storage and security, it took XT4 only 1.3723 minutes to break in, steal the gems, and exit. As he expected, the four known Alpha Team members were waiting for him outside.

"Didn't your manufacturer tell you it's not nice to steal without permission?" said Bulk.

"Hand over the gems," said Breez, "and let's see your hands—all four of them."

XT4 dropped the bag of jewels at his feet. "I have no interest in these crystalline objects," he said. "I came here in order to facilitate a meeting with Alpha Team. You are the robots designated Alpha Team, are you not?"

"That's the name," said Furno. "Are you looking to join up?"

"Negative," said XT4. "I represent the Citadel. There is a desire for negotiation with your organization. You will provide me with the coordinates of your headquarters so that we may send representatives to carry out these discussions as soon as possible."

Stormer laughed harshly. "Right. And your representatives will be unarmed, of course," he said, sarcasm in his voice. "We weren't built yesterday. You want to talk? Fine. Here are our terms: Our inner circle meets with your inner circle inside the Citadel. At that point, we'll present the conditions under which the Citadel will surrender its territories. Understand?"

XT4 tilted its head quizzically. "Naturally. I am conversant in all galactic languages and have a fifteenth-order intelligence. I am quite capable of comprehending your limited vocabulary. I will convey your message to my superiors. If your offer is accepted, we will signal you in an appropriate manner."

With those words, XT4 activated his boot jets

and soared off into the afternoon sky. The Heroes watched him go. When he was out of sight, Bulk said, "So we're demanding unconditional surrender, huh?"

"We want them curious," Stormer answered. "So curious they're willing to invite us inside their headquarters."

"With no intention of letting us leave," Furno pointed out. "You know that's part of the deal."

"But if we can find this world's version of our generator inside, we will be going," said Breez. "And we'll be heading back home."

"Here's hoping," said Bulk.

Far out in space, beyond the range of Von Nebula City's sensor array, a swarm of brains paused in mid-flight. Highly attuned to all environmental factors, they had sensed the presence of beings in this sector that did not belong in this reality. The scent of this distortion in the natural order of things had drawn them irresistibly to this spot.

In the far-flung region of space from which they originated, the brains had conquered every world. They had, at times, considered attacking this galaxy, but saw it as an insufficient challenge for their might. The suggestion that travel between realities might somehow be possible, though, had changed their collective minds.

What they wanted most could not be found in this universe . . . but perhaps it could be found in another.

Now that they were closer to their destination, they had been able to identify the elements that were out of tune with this dimension:

Stormer. Breez. Bulk. Furno.

No doubt these robots would, at some point, attempt to cross back to their own home reality. Before that happened, the brains would have wrested the secret of such travel from them and invaded this other dimension, in search of what they knew would make them invincible. Oh, and perhaps they would decimate this galaxy as well, just for practice. . . .

Well-satisfied with the way their plans were unfolding, the brains resumed their flight toward Von Nebula City. New worlds to conquer awaited them, and what more could a disembodied brain ask for?

5

The Heroes waited thirty-six hours to hear something from the Citadel. Von Nebula, Stormer assumed, was trying to make them worry. It was working.

If they figured out that there is no organization—just us four—they can come at us in force and that will be the end of everything, thought Stormer. *Our only hope is that there's just the tiniest seed of doubt—the thought that maybe, just maybe, there really is another syndicate out to take over.*

Not for the first time, Stormer found himself wondering about this universe. If there was another Von Nebula and another XT4 and another Jawblade, then wouldn't it follow there would be another Stormer and another Furno? Where were they while all this crime and corruption was going on? Had they gone into hiding, died fighting against it, or were they somewhere else, actively leading an underground resistance movement? He wished he had had more time with the Histotron to find out.

Bulk stepped into the doorway and knocked on the wall. "I think we got our signal."

Stormer got up and followed his old friend. To his surprise, he found a large water tank in the center of the room. Inside the tank, bound in chains, was Jawblade.

"Furno found it outside," Bulk explained. "They know where we are. But what's with fish-face here?"

"It's a gesture of good faith, or this world's version of one," Stormer answered. "Jawblade does crimes on the water. By taking him out of play, they're conceding that territory to us . . . or pretending to do so."

"I got it," said Bulk. "They want to show they're willing to negotiate."

"Right," answered Stormer. "Get the others. We're heading for the Citadel."

Everyone knew to expect Alpha Team, evidently. When Stormer and his crew arrived at the gates of the Citadel, the jolters guarding it opened the main doors. They did seem to spend a lot of time staring at Furno, though, as if shocked to see him free. Stormer wondered if the Furno of this reality was locked up behind these stone walls somewhere.

Part of the plan had hinged on Von Nebula wanting to intimidate these newcomers by having them see just how powerful and complex the Citadel was—by showing them its security features, and so on. It rapidly became apparent that they were not going to get a guided tour. Instead, they were herded into an elevator and brought directly to a large meeting chamber.

Stormer and his team stepped out of the lift and onto the stone floor. The first thing they noticed was that their footsteps were silent. Somehow, the rock had been engineered to absorb sound.

At a semicircular dais sat the inner circle of the Citadel — Speeda Demon, XT4, Core Hunter, Black Phantom, Toxic Reapa, and Von Nebula. Each of the members sat beneath a spotlight, except Von Nebula, who stayed in shadow. But even the darkness could not conceal his startled motion when he first saw Stormer.

"You wanted to see us," said Black Phantom. "If you have something to say, say it."

"I don't talk to henchbots," Stormer snapped. "I talk to the boss."

"Better watch your mouth . . . and your core," said Core Hunter. "Nobody tells the Citadel what to do."

"I'm pretty sure we just did," said Furno. "Otherwise, why are we here and not in some junk heap somewhere?"

"That is what I would like to know," grumbled

Toxic Reapa. "In the old days, I would have melted these upstarts down and laughed about it later. Now we treat them like honored guests."

Von Nebula's finger moved to a toggle switch. He flipped it and the floor opened beneath Toxic Reapa. The acidic villain vanished with a scream. The sound was cut off as the panel closed again.

"If I would do that to one of my inner circle, purely for speaking out of turn," said Von Nebula, "you would be wise to think about what I would do to you."

"Cut out the dramatics," said Stormer. "We're not here for a show."

"Very well," said Von Nebula. "XT4?"

XT4 rose. "An extensive search of all records in the known galaxy has resulted in no references to any organization known as 'Alpha Team.' Nor have encounters with any members of this organization been reported, other than the four we see before us. Conclusion: There is no such organization."

"Talk your way out of that," said Core Hunter.

Stormer had been prepared for something

like this. "We don't advertise," he shot back. "We started out small, sure, and we knew if we attracted your attention, we'd get crushed."

"So we worked behind the scenes," said Bulk. "A bribe here, a hijacking there, all little stuff you weren't likely to notice. Once we had enough credits and power, we made our move."

"You had your day," said Breez. "It's time for fresh oil."

"And your demands are?" asked Von Nebula.

"Nothing you can't meet," answered Stormer. "Alpha Team takes over the quadrant. Your structure stays in place, but you answer to us, and we take a fifty percent cut of the profits. In return, you get to continue managing your areas as you see fit, as long as the credits keep rolling in."

"What if we just vaporize you instead?" said Core Hunter.

Stormer chuckled. "Oh, you wouldn't want to do that. Trust me. You wouldn't want to feel what would come down on your head."

"Big talk," growled Black Phantom. "But I don't see any organization. I see four robots."

"And I don't see a 'Citadel,'" Stormer said. "I see a meeting room. How do I know this isn't just an impressive pile of rock with nothing inside it?"

"You could get to know the inside of it very well," said Von Nebula, making it very clear that it would not be as honored guests. "But before we proceed, I have a question you must answer—who *are* you?"

"My name is Stormer."

The words hung in the air for an electric moment. Then Von Nebula rose and leaned forward across the dais, just enough to make his form visible to his visitors. "You . . . are a liar," he hissed.

In their time, all the Heroes assembled had seen some pretty awful sights. It came with the job. Hero Factory had to face the things everyone else would be afraid of, but this . . . it took all their training to keep from shuddering with disgust.

Imagine a robot crushed by the sheer power of gravity, folded in on himself, and then abruptly unfolded by a gravitational backlash. Von Nebula's robot body had been compressed beyond all concept by a force powerful enough to trap light itself, then warped and distorted as he was restored to three-dimensional existence. It was like nothing anyone had ever seen before, and well beyond what any known science could repair. Von Ness had been a traitor . . . Von Nebula a master criminal . . . and now he was truly a monster.

Stormer kept his face rock solid, refusing to betray any of what he felt at the sight. He simply said, "You're wrong. I am who I say I am."

"Then, how?" Von Nebula shouted. "Who repaired you? Who could undo what I did to you? I must know!"

The other members of the inner circle looked at Von Nebula with undisguised fear. They had seen him angry before, plenty of times, but this seemed to go beyond that somehow. Black Phantom was slowly edging out of his chair, just in case Von Nebula's armored fist came down on the control panel and sent them all plummeting to their dooms.

Stormer, too, sensed that his old enemy was

on the edge. It wasn't the time to stoke his rage even hotter, or try to tell him the truth — that he wasn't the same Stormer this Von Nebula had fought before. *In fact, it might even be wiser,* Stormer thought, *to let him believe what he wants to believe.*

"Sometimes, amazing things can be accomplished if you know the right people," Stormer answered quietly. "We can talk about it . . . after we make a deal."

"You fool," spat Von Nebula. "Did you really think we were going to have a negotiation? You are here and you will stay here."

Sliding panels opened up in the walls all around the room. Jolters stepped through them, weapons trained on the four Heroes.

"Take them to the cells," ordered Von Nebula. "And tell Voltix to ready the interrogation chamber. I think they have stories to tell us."

Stormer and his team were marched out of the meeting room and herded toward the cells. "Well, that didn't go too well," said Furno under his breath.

"Actually, it did," said Stormer. "We're inside, where we needed to be, and right about now, Bulk is feeling really sick."

"Huh?"

Just behind Furno, Bulk suddenly doubled over in pain. When a jolter came to check on him, Bulk shot up and landed a rock-hard fist on the guard's helmet. That was the signal for the other Heroes to go into action. In the narrow hallway, the jolters couldn't use their weapons without risk of hitting each other. The Heroes made short work of them, leaving the entire guard unconscious in only a matter of seconds.

"Now we find the generator?" asked Breez. "If there is one, I mean."

"No," said Stormer. "Now we find the cells."

Seeing the puzzled look on Furno's face, he added, "In our world, we lock up criminals. In this world, they lock up heroes. So we're going to do a breakout of our own before we go home."

They weren't far from the cells, as it turned out. Bulk spotted two jolters on guard at the entrance to the wing. "Too long of a hallway to rush them," he said. "They'd cut us down before we got three steps."

"I might have an idea," said Furno. "When we came in, the guards were looking at me like I had two heads. Let's see how these guys react."

Furno stepped out into the hallway and walked straight toward the guards. They immediately aimed their weapons at him. One said, "Hey, how did you get out of your cell?"

"Wouldn't you like to know?" Furno shot back, smiling.

While one took up position behind Furno, the other opened the door to the jail wing. Neither of them saw Stormer come up behind them until it was too late. An instant later, they were both unconscious on the floor.

"My cell?" said Furno.

"Let's see," Stormer replied.

The four Heroes entered the cell block. Only about half of the cells were occupied, fighters for justice being in short supply in this reality. They had gone only a short distance when Furno found himself face-to-face with . . . William Furno.

William stood up from the cot in his cell. He stared at his double through the bars. "What kind of a trick is this?" he said. "You couldn't get me to betray my friends, so now you're going to use a double? And that Stormer — obviously none of you have seen him lately."

"We're not who you think we are," said Bulk. "We're friends."

Breez took the electronic key she had gotten off one of the guards and inserted it in the lock. The cell door swung open. "See? You're free."

"I don't believe you," said William. "This is another trap, like that story about the safe house."

Up to that point, Furno had been too shocked to say anything. Now he stepped forward, grabbed his double, and yanked him out of the cell. "Listen to me," said Furno. "We're here from . . . someplace else. We're trying to get back there, and if we do, it's going to be up to you and robots like you to bring this rotten Citadel down. So you can sit in there and be too scared to move, or you can go free the rest of the prisoners and make yourself useful! What's it going to be?"

William looked from Furno to Stormer to Bulk and Breez. Then he said, "All right, give me the key. But if this is a trick, trust me, I can make things very hot for you."

"Oh, just what we needed, two of them," grumbled Bulk.

"Let's get everyone else freed," said Stormer. "Breez, see if you can access the guards' computer station and get a layout of this place. We need to find whatever passes for a testing lab here."

"On it," said Breez.

"Hey," said Bulk. "You think there's another one of me?"

"I hope not," Stormer said with a smile. "I don't think any galaxy is big enough for two Bulks."

"Well, thanks," Bulk replied. "I think. Was that a compliment, or an insult?"

"Figure it out later, old friend," Stormer answered. "We have work to do."

In the Citadel control room, Voltix's board was lighting up, indicating mass escapes. What was going on down there? Whatever it was, he would put a stop to it before the inner circle found out about it. Black Phantom would like nothing better than to disgrace him and give his job to Splitface.

He was about to hit the alarm button that would summon all reserve guards when a cry from one of the technicians caught his attention.

"We have incoming from space!"

"What?" said Voltix. "What kind of incoming? Spaceships? Asteroids? What?"

"N-no, sir," came the answer. "They look like . . . brains!"

Got it!" said Breez.

Stormer rushed to her side. Sure enough, she had found a complete map of the Citadel. Outlined in red was a testing laboratory.

"Good work," said Stormer. "If it's anywhere, it's there."

He turned back to the assembled prisoners. Some he recognized from Hero Factory in his world, others he did not. But he knew they were all here for daring to stand up for what was right, in a universe that glorified what was wrong.

"I can't pretend to know what you've all been through," Stormer said. "But you have a second chance. Whether you want to fight or you just want to get as far from here as possible, you have the opportunity to do it right now. Guards are probably on their way, so you need to move. Good luck!"

The group headed for the exit. As William passed, Stormer put out a hand to stop him. "You mentioned Stormer," he said. "Do you know where he is . . . how he is?"

"I know," said Furno. "He said . . . he said he was going to try and find Makuro. Maybe he thought the one who started it all would be the only one who could help him. I doubt he ever found him — I doubt there was anything to find."

Stormer nodded and let him go with the others. "All right, let's get to the lab. It's time to get out of here, if we can."

They were on their way out the door when Voltix's voice rang through the Citadel communication system. "Alert Level Infrared! We have a possible alien invasion of Von Nebula City! All jolters report to stations. Aliens resemble organic brains. Set weapons for maximum charge."

"Brains?" said Bulk. "You don't think—?"

"What else could they be?" said Stormer grimly. "They attacked in our universe. It makes sense they would attack here, too."

Bulk had to agree. Back home, on multiple occasions, the Heroes had faced attacks by alien brains with the power to take over robot bodies. So far, they had been lucky, and even discovered a means of getting the brains to release their hold on a captive.

"Do you suppose anyone here knows how to deal with those things?" he asked Stormer.

"I doubt it," said the Alpha Team leader.

"It's not our universe," said Furno. "Is it really our problem?"

"We're Hero Factory," said Breez. "Our job doesn't end at the borders of our own dimension, does it?"

Stormer considered her words. There was no way of knowing if there was a generator here similar to theirs, or if there was, how long it would be intact for them to use. Taking time out to battle a brain invasion might cost them any chance they had of getting back home.

But Breez was right. This universe was not just full of Von Nebula and Splitface and robots like that. There were Heroes here, too, or at least beings who desperately wanted to be Heroes and were willing to risk imprisonment or worse. They deserved better than to wind up as host bodies for alien brains. Alpha Team knew the brains' weaknesses, at least some of them, and that knowledge gave them the responsibility to act.

"Breez, get me into the security feed," he ordered. "I want to see what's going on out there."

Out in the streets, Splitface and Thornraxx were rapidly discovering the answer to Stormer's question. Splitface hated working with the giant insect, who smelled bad and whose table manners were, if anything, even worse. But in a crisis like this, everyone had to listen to Voltix, like it or not.

Splitface knew what a brain looked like, or at least could guess. It would be relatively small, about the size of a piece of mass driver cannon ammunition. According to Voltix, these brains were mobile, but really, how fast could a brain be? His guess was, this whole thing was just a lot of noise to make Voltix and his jolters seem more important than they were.

Well, I'll blast the first little brain I see and bring it back and throw it on Voltix's desk, he said to himself. *Then we'll see who really saved this city.*

He peered around the hastily assembled barricade he and Thornraxx had thrown up. The streets were deserted. He was about ready to dismiss this whole thing as a false alarm when he saw them.

They weren't small, and they weren't slow. The brains were the size of some of the great cats he had seen in a zoo he robbed once, and each had six spiderlike legs. They also had two gossamer-thin wings sprouting from the folds on either side of their hemispheres.

The brains could fly.

"Hold these things off!" Splitface yelled to Thornraxx. "I have to alert the Citadel."

"You stay," Thornraxx buzzed. "I fly. Can get there faster."

"Miserable insect, do what I tell you!" yelled Splitface.

"You stay. You fight. If you run . . . you not get far."

It was already too late for either of them to get away. But the brains did not seem interested in them, strangely enough. They could have taken over the robots' bodies and gained their knowledge, but neither one seemed to be particularly intelligent. Most important, neither of the two was from another dimension.

No, hardly worth bothering with, the brains decided. They settled for firing bolts of concentrated mental energy, which caused both robots to collapse in a heap.

With that minor obstacle removed, they resumed their search for their four targets.

Inside the Citadel, chaos reigned. Jolters racing to defend the fortress had run right into escaped prisoners, and pitched battles were now being fought all over the lower floors. Meanwhile, the first of the brains had landed on the roof and were using their mental bolts to blast through the masonry.

Inside the cell block, Stormer and his team were watching through the Citadel's security cameras. The battle was not going well.

"Those *aren't* our brains," said Bulk. "Ours were smaller, didn't have wings, and couldn't blow stone to pieces just by looking hard at it."

"They must have developed in a different way in this universe," said Furno. "But they're still after the same thing."

"Are they?" said Breez. "I'm not so sure."

"What do you mean?" asked Stormer.

"I don't know, something doesn't feel right," said Breez. "This city is full of defensive strongpoints. In our universe, the brains would have overrun them and taken over as many minds as they could. Here — well, look for yourselves."

Breez punched up a series of security camera feeds from around Von Nebula City. They all showed the same thing: brains bypassing strongpoints, either by going around or flying over. Then Breez switched to a wide-angle view from a satellite camera. Now it was obvious that all of the brains were converging on the Citadel.

"That settles it," said Bulk. "Next time, I pick the vacation spot."

"Why here? Do they see the Citadel as an obstacle to conquest, like they did Hero Factory? Or is that too simple an explanation?" wondered Stormer.

"Why don't we go ask them?" suggested Furno. "They're knocking on the roof."

"Let's do it," said Stormer.

Von Nebula could hear the brains blasting away one floor above him. The rest of the inner circle was busy attending to the defense of the Citadel's more sensitive locations, at his command. He preferred to face these invaders alone and find out why they dared attack his fortress.

He stood in his chamber, his eyes riveted to the ceiling as a spiderweb of cracks began to form. Then, masonry began to rain down around him and he could see the sky above. An instant later, two brains flew through the opening and hovered in the air above him.

"Can you speak?" Von Nebula asked. There was no fear in his voice. He could, after all, open a black hole faster than they could likely react, and see them drawn into its depths.

The brains seemed surprised that he had spoken to them, as opposed to either attacking or running. He saw the slightest furrow in one of the brains and then heard its voice in his head.

The words were muffled by heavy static, trans-mitted as they were from the electrical storm within an organic brain.

We can understand . . . and think *to you, robot.*

"Then tell me why you're here," said Von Nebula. "Why are you attacking?"

We seek the Four who will show us the way.

Von Nebula couldn't make any sense of that. He tried again. "I am a very powerful robot. Perhaps I could help you find what it is you're seeking . . . if you stop harming my servants."

Your mind holds the knowledge? Then we will take it from you.

One of the brains descended, hovering just above Von Nebula's head. Raising his Orb Staff a little tighter, Von Nebula prepared to unleash its power.

"On our world, we don't take things we want," Von Nebula lied. "We trade for them. And if you can steal knowledge from a robot mind, then I believe you have something I want."

Speak.

"I'll help you find the Four, and in return . . .

you drain certain knowledge from the mind of a robot, knowledge that I must have."

The brains were silent for a moment. Then —

Agreed.

"Good. So who are these Four that you're looking for?"

We know their names only: Stormer, Bulk, Breez, Furno.

Von Nebula smiled. It seemed that he and the brains had more in common than even he had imagined.

"Do you hear something?" asked Bulk. He and the other Heroes had made their way almost to the top floor of the Citadel. Resistance had been light, since most of the jolters were focused on defending the building from an external threat.

"No," said Furno.

"Neither do I," said Bulk. "It sounds like the fighting's stopped."

"You think the brains won?" asked Breez.

"I have a feeling somehow we're in more trouble than we were before," said Bulk. "Don't ask me why I think that—I just do."

Stormer had learned a long time ago to listen to Bulk's hunches. "What do you suggest?"

"That we're quick and quiet," Bulk answered. "Let's not go charging in."

The four Heroes continued their journey upward. Rather than risk taking elevators, they were climbing up maintenance ladders. At the very top of the building, there was a locked hatch. A quick application of heat from Furno and it was able to be opened.

Furno pushed it ajar just a crack and peered around. There was no sign of any battle, but there was a huge hole in the roof. He waved for the others to follow him and then crawled out onto the rooftop.

Staying low, the Heroes moved to the edge of the hole. Looking down, they saw Von Nebula with two brains hovering near him. The villain seemed to be talking to himself.

"What way are they supposed to show you? . . . Because I need to know, if I am going to help you . . . Why are you interested in those four specifically?"

"Has he gone nuts?" Bulk whispered. "I mean, more nuts than usual?"

"They're talking to him," Breez whispered back. "They must be, via thought-projection. Wait, what's he saying now?"

"What do you mean, you no longer need my help?" Von Nebula said loudly. "What do you—nearby? Where?"

Stormer immediately did the math and realized what was going on. "Run! Back into the building!"

His realization came too late. The brains had already soared up through the hole. Before the Heroes could react, they had all been felled by bolts of mental energy.

Von Nebula reached the roof in time to see them fall. "I see," he said. "You will keep our bargain, however."

We have no need of a bargain with you now, the brains sent to him.

Von Nebula gestured with his staff. The beginnings of a black hole began to form in the air near the brains. "I said, you will keep our bargain, won't you?"

The brains considered their choice: be stubborn and be crushed by gravity, or go along with what this annoying robot wanted. It was a simple decision to make.

Very well. We will gain the knowledge we need, and you will gain the knowledge you need. Of course, there may be little left of the target's mind when we are done.

"That," Von Nebula said, "concerns me not at all."

When Stormer woke up, he was in the prison repair bay, chained to a table. His fellow Alpha Team members were nowhere to be seen. A half dozen brains hovered near the ceiling. Von Nebula stood over him, his grotesque face twisted into a smile.

"You should have stayed in whatever hole you crawled into, Stormer," said Von Nebula. "Well, this time, you will not be coming back."

"I'm not . . . who you think I am," said the Alpha Team leader. "I'm not your Stormer."

"It's too late for lies," Von Nebula whispered. "It's too late for anything. When my new allies are done with you, I will display you like a trophy in the heart of the Citadel, as a warning to other fools who do not know their place."

The black-armored villain looked up at the brains. "Do it. Now."

One of the brains flew down from the ceiling. Before Stormer could say or do anything, it had fastened itself upon his head. His robot body spasmed as knowledge drained from his mind like a river emptying into a vast ocean.

At the same time, he could see into the minds of the brains—see their passage through space, their conquests of world after world, for no apparent reason other than pure pleasure. Unlike the brains in his universe, which he was sure were a tool of some other entity, these were nomadic warriors who had evolved to survive in the vacuum of space. Nor could they control another being's mind for an indefinite period of time, for their hosts burned out swiftly. They had no interest in ruling over others, as Von Nebula did, but simply spreading devastation and destruction wherever they went. At least, that was how it appeared on the surface. . . .

Yet, as their mental probes of Stormer went deeper, he found that he was able to read their thoughts at a deeper level as well. He could see vast factories filled with robot bodies being assembled, each one designed to house a brain in its head and spinal column. These robots would have no independent wills of their own, but exist solely as armored exoskeletons for the brains. The creatures' last vulnerability—their organic bodies—would cease to be a weakness worth worrying about.

With strong limbs and deft hands, the brains would be able to build battle machines that could overrun even the most heavily fortified worlds.

Everything they were now would be multiplied a hundredfold.

There was only one problem. The technology they needed to seamlessly link their bodies to a robot did not exist in this universe. Every attempt they had made up to now had failed miserably. But Stormer knew—and now they knew, as well—that what they needed could be found somewhere else. It was contained in another reality, in a place called Hero Factory.

Now all they had to do was get there.

Abruptly, the brain broke the linkage. Stormer gasped, but did not open his optic receptors. The brains, and perhaps Von Nebula as well, would expect him to be a mindless hunk of metal after that experience. For reasons he couldn't imagine, his mind was still intact. That was a secret he intended to keep for a while longer.

It is done, the brain messaged to its fellow invaders, as well as Von Nebula. *We have found the way.*

"And what about what I was seeking?"

demanded Von Nebula. "I crushed Stormer once before, yet here he is, intact and whole. Whoever did that for him—"

Can do that for you, robot? the brain finished for him. *Perhaps that would be the case, if he were the Stormer you had defeated. But he is not. You have been chasing a ghost, Von Nebula, for this Stormer comes from another dimension.*

"That . . . cannot be," said Von Nebula. "Two Stormers? That would mean . . ."

Two Von Nebulas, the brain agreed. *Only, in that reality, he never attained the heights you did . . . or paid the price you have paid for your ambition.*

Von Nebula's mind whirled. Somewhere in the endless array of parallel worlds, there existed a Von Nebula who had never tried to merge his weapon with himself, never been warped and twisted by it. If he had not become the head of the Citadel and master of much of a galaxy, he at least was whole. Von Nebula thought about this double living in another universe, and a surge of emotion threatened to overwhelm him.

He hated this twin he had never met. Even more than that, he hated the idea that this other Von Nebula might one day follow this Stormer here. An intact, undamaged Von Nebula could drive him from his seat of power in the Citadel . . . and that power was all he had left.

The brains interrupted his thoughts. *Take us to the generator, robot.*

"The generator?"

That is the way. The gateway to the other reality, the brains transmitted to the robot's mind.

Of course, thought Von Nebula. *There must be a counterpart to the power source we are testing for the Citadel in Stormer's world. That is how those four robots got here—and now the brains want to use it to invade their reality.*

Von Nebula's first instinct was to step aside and let the brains have what they wanted. What did he care about some other universe? Let it be destroyed. But then he reminded himself that an important decision should not be made in haste. He needed time to consider.

"I do have such a machine," he conceded. "But it is not completed yet. To use it now would mean your destruction."

The brains regarded him with suspicion. At the same time, they could not take him over to discover if he was lying, because they might burn him out. They still needed Von Nebula to work the machine. Nothing in Stormer's mind had told them *how* to use it to get to another dimension.

Make it work, the brains projected.

All in good time, thought Von Nebula to himself. *All in good time.*

Stormer was tossed into a cell by the jolters. He made no effort to resist them, simply stared at the floor. Breez, in the cell next to him, gasped at the sight.

"What did they do to him?" she said. "He looks . . . mindless."

"I'll tear them apart!" said Bulk. "You hear me, you piles of space junk? When I get out of here, I'm going to pound you into metal scraps!"

Furno felt the same rage Bulk did, but he knew what Stormer would say: "Think with your head, not with your Hero Core." Von Nebula and his gang were only a small part of the problem. The brains were the real threat, and none of them had any idea yet how to deal with them.

"We'll . . . do what we can for Stormer," he said. "First, we have to get out of here. If Von Nebula has teamed up with the brains, this world is in more trouble than maybe anyone can handle. But we have to try. It's what Stormer would have wanted."

"Are the guards gone?" asked Bulk.

Breez peered through the bars of her cell door. "There's only one outside the main door. I guess they're still fighting the prisoners we set free."

"Okay, we don't have a key, so we'll just have to use brute strength on these cells," Bulk replied. "On the count of three, give it all you've got. One . . . two . . ."

"Three."

The voice belonged to Stormer, who had just gotten to his feet. He threw the door of his cell open and walked out.

"Stormer?!"

"You're all right?"

"How did you get free?"

"Apparently, they don't bother to lock your

door if they think your mind's burned out," Stormer explained. "Now, hang on."

Stormer snuck up to the main door that led out to the corridor. Flattening himself against the wall, he cried out, "Brains! Brains! They're breaking in through the walls!"

The guard turned to look, but saw nothing through the little window into the cell block. He had to open the door. As soon as he did, Stormer took him out with a quick blow. Then he wrested the electronic key from the fallen guard and set his friends free.

"Listen close," Stormer said. "There *is* a generator here. We can try to use it to get back, but I'll have to stay behind to destroy it once the rest of you are gone. No matter what, we can't let the brains get their claws on it."

"So that's it?" said Bulk. "We just run out and leave you? Not going to happen."

"I wasn't asking," said Stormer. "Think about it: If the brains evolved into what we're seeing in this universe, maybe they will do the same in ours. If that happens, Hero Factory will need the three of you to help fight them off. I'll do what I can here to mount a defense."

No one liked the sound of that. Bulk had already decided that, if it came down to it, he would throw Stormer into the generator field and stay behind himself. Furno and Breez were both thinking basically the same thing.

Together, they moved out, heading for the lab. When they got there, they saw Core Hunter engaged in what seemed to be a heated argument with the two brains guarding the door. He wanted in, and they weren't about to let him pass. After a minute more, he turned and stalked down the corridor.

As he rounded a corner, Bulk grabbed him and clamped a hand over his mouth. "Keep quiet, you. In any universe, I'd bash you just for fun."

Core Hunter calculated the four-against-one odds and stopped struggling. Stormer talked to him in a harsh whisper. "You have a computer in your head, Core Hunter, use it. Do you really think those . . . things . . . are going to stop once they get what they want here? Or are they going to bring the Citadel down just because they can?"

Core Hunter shrugged off Bulk's grip. The Hero gave him a warning glance as he released his hold. "And what's your big idea, Stormer?" said the villain. "The four of you make all the brains go away?"

"We need our weapons," said Stormer. "They were taken when we got captured on the roof. Where are they stored?"

"Right, 'cause you're going to save us all," Core Hunter snapped. "I heard all about you four. Back where you come from, you hound and harass robots like me. Why should I help you?"

Stormer grabbed Core Hunter by the shoulders and slammed him into the wall. "You haven't seen what I've seen! Those creatures destroy—that's all they live for. You have one chance to survive what's going to happen here, and that's to help us!"

It was the truth, and Stormer knew it now. The brains wouldn't leave the generator in the hands of the Citadel, not knowing what it could do—and they wouldn't be content to just destroy the machine. They would lay waste to the entire planet as soon as they had the means to get where they wanted to go.

Fortunately, this Core Hunter was fundamentally no different from Core Hunter back home: He wanted to live. Without a word, he led the Heroes to a small armory in which their weapons were locked up. Once they had their equipment back in hand, Core Hunter said, "Now what?"

"We need to get into that lab," said Furno. "You were trying to get in, so you must have a pass."

"That's top security," Core Hunter replied. "And how are you going to get past the brains?"

"We're not," said Stormer. "We're going through them."

The five returned to the lab corridor. As the Heroes hid out of sight, Core Hunter approached the brains. "I spoke to Von Nebula," he said. "He said you don't have the authority to keep inner circle members out . . . if you have an issue, take it up with him . . . now, out of the way."

The brains didn't agree with that idea, but they apparently were willing to debate it with Von Nebula. With Core Hunter in the lead, they started back down the hallway. As soon as they had passed, Stormer stepped out into the corridor and fired his plasma weapon twice, bringing the brains down.

"They're still alive," said Breez. "Just stunned."

"What's the matter with you?" said Core Hunter. "Kill them!"

"We don't do that," said Furno. "That's why we're who we are, and you're who you are. And that's why" — Furno lashed out with the flat of his sword, knocking Core Hunter unconscious. — "you're still alive, too."

Taking his lab pass, the Heroes entered the lab. There was the generator, looking much like the one back at Hero Factory that had sent them on this mad journey.

"All right, we have to assume it was sabotaged and that's why it malfunctioned," said Stormer. "Bulk, do you think you can take a shot at figuring out what was broken, and how to fix it?"

"Sure," said the powerful Hero. "If there's one thing I know about, it's breaking things."

Bulk crouched down and examined the machine, with Breez looking over his shoulder. After a few minutes, he said, "Well, I see one problem. This thing isn't going to work."

"What?"

Bulk reached into the inner workings of the machine and took out part of a cylinder of metal. It had been neatly cut in half. "This is the amelium cylinder—you know, the thing that keeps the whole works from melting a hole down to the core of the planet. Somebody took half of it with them, and without that, turning this thing on would be suicide for the whole city."

Stymied again, thought Stormer. *It's as if something in this universe wants evil to win.*

"Can't we jury-rig something?" asked Furno.

"Sure," said Bulk. "That is, if you happen to

be carrying a rare metal on you that half the galaxy would give their logic circuits for."

"Maybe—" Breez began.

Her idea was never given voice. The door to the lab slid open to reveal the twisted form of Von Nebula. In his hand, he held the other half of the cylinder. "Looking for this, Heroes?"

All four turned, weapons at the ready. Von Nebula simply laughed. "Go ahead. What can you do to me that is worse than what has already been done?"

"We can make sure that whatever happens in this city, you won't be around to enjoy it," Bulk growled.

"You wrong me, you brainless buffoon," Von Nebula replied. "I am not here to gloat. I am here to state simple facts. You are trapped here without this half of the cylinder; if you try to take it from me, I will simply destroy it and you will never see your home again. Or . . ."

"Or?" said Stormer.

Von Nebula gave a terrible smile. "You can become my allies."

All four Heroes started protesting at once, but Von Nebula silenced them with a gesture. "I find myself in a most difficult position," he said. "If I let the brains travel to your universe, they will surely destroy Hero Factory. Normally, I would not care about that—but from what they tell me, I think it is likely that without Hero Factory, my counterpart in your reality will rise to power. I will not have that intact . . . *mockery* of me winning in the end."

Von Nebula drew himself up to his full height, an act that was obviously painful for him. "At the same time, to defy the brains is to invite destruction of the Citadel and all that I have built here. I cannot abide that, either. That leaves only one alternative: eliminate the brains, here and now. For that, I need your help."

"Why not just ask your crew of crooks?" asked Furno.

"Because there are some avenues closed even to them," Von Nebula said. He held out the half-cylinder to Stormer. "A gesture of good faith, and perhaps an explanation — please look at the maker's mark."

Stormer did as he was asked. There were precious few robots back home who could work with amelium. It was an extremely fragile and, under certain conditions, volatile metal. Those who could manipulate it left their mark with pride, a unique signature that told the galaxy what they had done.

It was tiny, almost microscopic, but it was there. And it made Stormer's core go cold.

"When . . . ?" he asked.

"Three years ago," Von Nebula answered. "Since then, he has not been . . . cooperative. Perhaps you can change that."

"The Histotron said he disappeared, presumed deactivated."

Von Nebula gave a dark chuckle. "The Histotron, Stormer, says what I want it to say."

"Would one of you give the rest of us a clue what you're talking about?" demanded Bulk.

Stormer handed him the portion of amelium.

There, carved on the end, was the maker's mark of Akiyama Makuro, would-be founder of Hero Factory.

In the end, it was decided that Stormer would go alone. The other three Heroes would stay behind to guard the lab, with Bulk keeping the severed piece of cylinder. Von Nebula knew they would not leave without their leader, but he extracted a promise from Bulk to destroy the amelium rather than let the brains get it.

The Hero and villain did not take the elevators, for fear the brains would notice their movements. Instead, they went back down the maintenance ladders until they reached the ground floor. There Von Nebula opened a secret passage that led to a winding stairway. It went down beyond the basements and sub-basements and into the bowels of the city itself. Stormer felt as if they had left the world of the living behind and were now in some dark limbo where the shades of robots past flitted about the shadows.

Down a long, dank corridor that stank of old machine oil and rust, they came to Makuro's cell. Inside was the huddled figure of the great inventor. Von Nebula rapped on the door. "You have a visitor."

"Go away," said Makuro, in a voice grown hoarse from disuse. "I want nothing from you and will do nothing for you. I fashioned the amelium only so you would not destroy this city with your 'engineering marvel.' Go away!"

Stormer took the key from Von Nebula and unlocked the cell door. "Mr. Makuro, I'm . . . a friend."

The sight of the white-armored robot made Makuro back away into a corner. "Who are you? What are you? How dare you wear the face of a true hero?" Makuro pointed to Von Nebula, who stood in the doorway. "He thinks he ruined Stormer! But I saved him! I was able to smuggle the plans out to him, so he would be better than before! One day, he will return for me, you'll see."

"This was a mistake," said Von Nebula. "He is raving."

"Keep quiet," snapped Stormer. He crouched down in front of Makuro. "Sir, I am not the Stormer you know—I am from a different universe, one where your dream of Hero Factory came true. The city—*your* city—is in terrible danger, and you may be the only one who can help us."

Makuro stared hard at Stormer for a long time. Then he said flatly, "It's a trick, and not a very good one. Go away."

"Your second wave," Stormer said. "After Alpha Team, you had planned another group—Rocka, Evo, Surge, Breez. You never got to build them. In my world, you did. I have been proud to serve with each and every one of them. Where I come from, you may be the greatest Hero of all."

"Rocka . . . Evo . . . Von Ness never knew those names," Makuro said softly, almost as if he were talking to himself. "Neither did Stormer.

I never told anyone. How could you know, unless . . . ?"

A light flickered in Makuro's eyes. He believed.

Stormer watched as the old robot sat up straight, looking as if he were shedding years as he did so. When Makuro spoke again, his voice was stronger.

"Tell me everything—and find me a place to work."

8

In the far corners of the galaxy, the brains were known for many things — ruthlessness, savagery, cunning, and a complete lack of mercy among them. Patience was not on that list.

It had been hours since they had drained the mind of the one called Stormer, and yet the generator was still not operational. Although many of those who had been held prisoner in the Citadel had managed to escape, for the most part all resistance had crumbled. But the brains were not about occupying territory — they preferred to flatten it. This endless waiting for the chance to invade a new universe was starting to get annoying.

Finally, one of the brains was dispatched to the lab to check on progress. When it arrived, it found that the two members of its species assigned to guard the room were missing. Moving closer, it heard the voices of some of the Four behind the lab door.

We are betrayed, it thought.

Flying as fast as it could in the winding corridors, it went to alert its leaders. The Citadel, and everyone in it, was about to pay for daring to defy the swarm.

William Furno and his fellow escapees made their way to the waterfront. The jolters stationed in the area had been pulled back to defend the Citadel, and the brains had largely bypassed the area. It gave the group of fugitives a chance to rest and decide what to do next.

"We have to go back," said William.

"Are you crazy?" said one of the ex-prisoners. "I never want to go near that place again."

"Those four helped us," William persisted. "We can't just abandon them."

"Listen," said William's best friend, Jimi Stringer, "Even with the gear we took off the jolters, we haven't got the power to storm the Citadel. Plus, those brains are still in there! All we'd get is wiped out."

William knew Stringer was right. But from the time he was created, he had dreamed of being a real Hero. As a member of Alpha Team, he had been ready to take on the universe. Thanks to Von Ness, that dream got destroyed. Maybe this was his last chance to make it real.

"You guys can stay here, or try to find your way out of the city," William said at last. "I'm going back. It's what Heroes are supposed to do."

Stringer looked at his friend, wondering if he was the bravest robot he had ever met or the craziest. Then he flipped open a compartment on his belt and took out a small, black device. William recognized it right away as their old Alpha Team communicator.

"I kept this all these years," Stringer said.

"Don't know why. The jolters never found it . . . probably would have thought it was a useless piece of junk, anyway. But if you're going back into action . . . you should have it."

William took it, feeling the rush of memories again—his first days on the team, their early missions, the hope they all had for the future. Feeling the same sense of wonder he did ages ago, he activated the communicator.

There was a loud hiss of static that lasted a long while. Then a voice came through the tiny speaker, a voice from the past—

"Who's there?" it said. "Is someone on this frequency? Identify yourselves."

Impossible. . . thought William. *It . . . it can't be.*

Stringer and the others went dead silent, staring at the communicator like it had just turned into a serpent. Hesitantly, William pressed the "Send" button and said, "Hello? This is William Furno. Please acknowledge and . . . and identify yourself."

The next moment seemed to take a year to

go by. Then the voice said, "Furno? Furno, this is Preston Stormer. Where are you? What's happening? Report."

"Stormer!" William said, grinning. "We thought you were — well, we were wrong! I can't believe — "

"Neither can I," said Preston. "Who's with — no, wait, that can come later. Just . . . just give me the situation."

William explained everything he could, as quickly as he could. When he was done, Preston Stormer said, "Of course we're going back. We couldn't be Heroes and do any less."

"We?" asked William.

"Give me your coordinates," said Preston. "Mr. Makuro told me to stay out of sight, that Von Nebula would never stop hunting for me. The few attempts I made to escape the city failed. I've been waiting for a call from Alpha Team for all these years. . . ."

"Then maybe it's time that team lived again," said William.

9

I cannot do very much without a brain to examine, you understand," said Makuro. He had been puttering around in an auxiliary lab for the last fifteen minutes, piecing together components into a construct that made no sense to Von Nebula or Stormer.

"Can you help, or not?" said Von Nebula. "We have no time to waste on eccentric inventors past their prime."

"My prime," said Makuro, soldering two wires together, "was spent in one of your cells. I had a great deal of time to think about robotic life and organic life. Although one has a computer mind and the other a far more mysterious one, in the end, the two are not so very different. I believe I have the answer."

Makuro tried to fit one last piece into what was now obviously a weapon. It didn't want to fit, so he pounded it a few times until it did. Then he held it out to Stormer with pride.

"Low-emission beta waves," Makuro said, as if that explained everything.

"Which means . . . ?" said Stormer.

"Organic brains have different wave frequencies . . . at least, that is my theory. If I am right, low-emission beta waves are most frequently present when a being is active, stressed, alert — as your enemies would be in battle. This machine will jam those waves. If it works, they will drop like rocks."

"If," repeated Von Nebula.

"It's more than we had before," said Stormer. He turned to Von Nebula. "Makuro stays free, or I make sure the brains get you before bothering to test this thing."

"Agreed," said Von Nebula. "The days when he was a threat are long over."

Makuro chuckled. "Don't be so sure, you metal mistake. An old robot can still surprise you."

Stormer, Von Nebula, and Makuro were on their way to the upper levels when Bulk's call came in. "We've got trouble, Chief."

"What's the matter?" said Stormer.

"The brains want into the lab. We've beaten back the first bunch, but there's a lot of them."

Von Nebula activated his wrist communicator. "Speeda Demon, report."

"Brains are moving toward the Citadel from all over the city," Speeda Demon replied. "It looks like they're massing for another attack. I don't like the looks of it."

"I didn't ask for your opinion," snapped Von Nebula. "Send all available jolters to the lab section. Tell them if they don't stop the brains, I'll have them disassembled . . . slowly. Out."

He turned to Makuro. "This weapon had better work."

"It will, it will," Makuro assured him. "But . . . it was designed for a few brains at a time, not hundreds at once. You're going to need some way to divert their attention so you can pick them off."

The three raced up to the lab level. The first thing they saw when they got there was the unconscious bodies of Voltix and his jolters littering the hallway. The brains had been expecting their attack, and none had made it within twenty feet of the lab door.

Stormer spotted six brains blasting at that doorway with their mental bolts. They had already managed to sear a large hole in the metal. He fired the jammer in their direction. In a split second, all six had dropped to the ground and lay still.

"Are they dead?" asked Von Nebula.

"Asleep," said Makuro.

"You always were too merciful," sneered the head of the Citadel.

Stormer looked through the gap in the door. "Bulk, take both halves of the cylinder and let's head for the roof. They can come at us from both sides down here."

Bulk, Breez, and Furno exited the lab. If they were shocked to see Makuro, as they surely were, they kept it to themselves. There was a job to do.

The roof afforded a wonderful view of just how bad things were. A recovered Core Hunter was leading a desperate battle against the brains that were flooding toward the Citadel from all parts of Von Nebula City. A unit of jolters had succeeded in driving some of the brains out of the upper floors, but had lost almost all their robots doing it. Anyone could see the defenders were being overwhelmed.

"You have the weapon!" Von Nebula shouted. "Use it!"

Before Stormer could answer, Von Nebula had wrestled the jammer away from him and fired it at the swarm of brains down below. The weapon downed five or six, but there was a cost: It had attracted the attention of the rest of the brains to the roof.

"Now you've done it," said Bulk. "We had a nice little party going on up here, and now they're going to crash it . . . and us."

The brains were flying up toward the roof in a mass. The weapon that had hurt them was there; the Four were there; that was where the final battle would be fought.

"Get ready, Heroes," said Stormer. "Take down as many of them as you can."

The brains rose to the edge of the roof and beyond, blotting out the sun, ready to surge forward and attack. Then something totally unexpected happened, something that had not occurred in this universe for many years—

This world's Alpha Team attacked!

A mammoth explosion tore through the swarm, sending the brains scattering in multiple directions. Through the smoke and dust, Stormer saw an amazing sight. It was himself, the Preston Stormer of this dark mirror world, leading his fellow Heroes in an assault on the aliens. His legs had been replaced, his upper body now fused to a large, square weapons platform capable of jet flight and bristling with lasers and concussion missiles. Behind him came William Furno, Jimi Stringer, and countless others Stormer recognized — and some he didn't — all riding sky sleds into battle.

"You see?" Makuro said to Von Nebula. "I told you I fixed him. I taught him how to build the sleds, too . . . and he had plenty of time to make them, didn't he?"

Breez saw the look on Von Nebula's face — fury mixed with fear mixed with pure shock. She took advantage of the moment to bring the edge of her hand down on Von Nebula's wrist, making him drop the jammer. Furno grabbed it before it hit the ground.

"We've got a break!" shouted Stormer. "Hit them hard!"

Von Nebula City, and the galaxy that surrounded it, had seen many battles in its history. Most had been fought over territory or money or just out of anger, by robots who had no interest in anything other than themselves. No one had ever seen anything quite like this before: two groups of Heroes, the same but worlds apart, risking their lives to save those who had persecuted, oppressed, and jailed them.

For this world's Preston and his team, it was like being reborn. They used their speed and maneuverability to split the brains up into smaller groups, so that Furno could drop them with the jammer. Watching William execute an incredible double barrel roll, Furno said, "Wow, I'm pretty good."

"Yeah, yeah," said Bulk, hurling a piece of masonry at an oncoming brain. "When we get home, I'll buy you a mirror."

Slowly, the tide of battle was turning. Using Makuro's weapon, they were cutting down the numbers of the brains. For the aliens, retreat was not an option. They fought on, downing some Heroes before falling themselves.

Only one robot was paying no attention to the battle: Von Nebula. His attention was fixed solely on Preston Stormer, the Hero who in his mind had condemned him to a life as a distorted creature. Von Nebula no longer cared about the brains, or the Citadel, or anything else in existence. All that mattered was that Preston Stormer had to be destroyed.

Von Nebula raised his Black Hole Orb Staff and unleashed its terrible energies at his hated enemy. Both Stormers saw this at the same time. One fired his plasma weapon, the other a laser, striking the energies of the staff simultaneously.

It was a devastating combination. Blocked by the forces of plasma and laser light, the black hole power fed back into the staff, and from the staff to its wielder. Before the shocked eyes of all, Von Nebula began to fold in on himself, caught in the crushing grip of intense gravity. If he cried out, no one could hear it, for no sound could escape the black hole that was consuming him.

The villain shrank down, down, compressed by the same energies he had used so often for evil. And it did not stop—not until Von Nebula, the unquestioned leader of a whole sector of the galaxy, had become the size of a micron, then even smaller than that, beyond microscopic. All that was left was his staff, which clattered to the ground.

There was no time to feel revulsion or relief or, for those with more generous spirits, even to mourn. There were still brains that had to be defeated.

The fight finally ended the only way it could, as Heroes of the present and Heroes of the past met and shook hands over a now-still battlefield.

After it was all over, they assembled in the lab. Furno welded the two pieces of amelium together, under Makuro's supervision, and Bulk inserted it into the generator. He had made the "repairs" he felt needed to be done to make it malfunction in the right way. Now it was time for good-byes.

"Come back with us," said Stormer. "You would be honored where we come from. Our universe believes in Heroes."

"That's because of what you and your friends

have done," said Preston. "We have to earn our own honors, right here, starting with dismantling the Citadel and its whole rotten empire."

It was a real possibility now. Von Nebula was gone, the inner circle and the jolters decimated by the brains' attack. Word was spreading among the citizens of Von Nebula City about just who had saved them from the alien menace.

"And you?" Stormer asked Makuro.

"This is my second chance to create the Hero Factory I always dreamed of," Makuro replied. "It's a second chance for all of us . . . thanks to you. I hope my counterpart in your universe knows just how fortunate he is."

"We'll be destroying this generator as soon as you leave," said Preston. "I don't think you need any unwelcome visitors."

"Maybe we'll find some other way to cross over," said Bulk. "I'd like to come back here, see how you're doing."

"You would always be welcome," said William.

Bulk turned to Furno. "Why don't *you* stay

and we'll take *him* back with us? He's a lot more polite."

Furno smiled. "He's been through enough. Poor 'bot doesn't need hanging-around-with-you on top of it."

All of those who weren't headed back to Hero Factory's world filed out of the lab. Bulk triggered the generator. The hum turned into a whine as the power built up and ran out of control, for a second time. . . .

And then they were gone.

Epilogue

Perjast woke up in the repair bay. He couldn't move. At first, he thought it was the result of some systems malfunction. Then he realized he was strapped down to the cot.

He opened his optic sensors. Staring down at him were Stormer, Furno, Breez, and Bulk.

"Uh-oh," said Perjast.

"You got that right," said Bulk.

It didn't take much interrogation to get Perjast to confess that he had been sent to meet with Karter and was smuggling tech at the time. Even he didn't know what he had been carrying, nor had he known that his systems were rigged to shut down so that he would wind up in the repair bay.

"Karter," said Furno. "I should have guessed."

"Anybody up for a game of 'bounce the spy'?" asked Bulk.

"I might have a better idea," said Breez. "He thinks he destroyed us . . . so let him."

"What have you got cooking in your computer brain?" asked Bulk.

"Just this—when we got back, Zib said this whole place was evacuated. Once they realized there wasn't going to be an explosion, they brought everyone, Heroes and prisoners, back. So what if, next time, they couldn't evacuate?"

Bulk smiled. "I like your style, Breez."

"Let's find Zib," said Stormer. "We have a Hero Factory to destroy."

The alarm woke Karter up from a sound rest and recharge. *What, again?* he thought. *Someone else must have had the same idea I did.*

He sat up to see Zib scurrying down the hallway. "Hey!" Karter shouted. "What's going on here?"

Zib skidded to a halt. "It's that generator — we thought everything was all right, but the effect was just delayed! It's leaking energy, and the radiation is eating through everything in Hero Factory."

Karter jumped to his feet. "Then get me out of here! We have to evacuate!"

Zib shook his head sadly. "I'm afraid none of us are going anywhere. The radiation has already reached the hangars. All the Hero craft are inoperable. We're stranded here."

Without waiting for Karter's reply, Zib hurried on. Karter turned his back to the security camera and slid one fingertip gently aside, exposing a micro communicator. "This is Karter," he whispered urgently into the tiny speaker.

"Priority! If you are receiving me, come in!"

"We are receiving you," a voice crackled back. "What do you want?"

"Listen to me! Hero Factory is about to be destroyed by radiation from the generator I sabotaged. There's no way to do an evacuation. You need to get me out of this place."

"And how would we do that?"

"Don't play games!" Karter snarled. "You have credits, you have ships — you could break me out in the confusion."

"That would involve too much risk. We do not wish to risk exposure."

"You can't just leave me here! No one would ever know you were involved!" said Karter. "After all, everyone else here is going to be fried."

"Well, that's a pleasant thought."

Karter whirled to see Stormer, Bulk, Furno, and Breez standing in his cell. Stormer walked up to him, grabbed his wrist, and brought the built-in communicator up to his mouth.

"Now, you listen, whoever you are," Stormer said. "You tried, and you failed. Now Hero

Factory is going to come for you. Do you understand me?"

"You overestimate yourselves," came the reply. "And you underestimate us. We are beyond your reach. Your only link to us is Karter."

"And how long do you think he's going to stay loyal, now that he knows you were willing to leave him here to die?"

"Oh, we are willing to do a great deal more than that."

Karter suddenly spasmed. There was a harsh sizzle of unleashed energy and the smell of burning wires. Then the spy fell to the ground, dead.

"Good-bye, Stormer," came the voice over the communicator. "Until we meet again."

On a far-off frontier world, a crimson robot switched off a communicator. This had been a most disturbing day, and so he punched in the code for some gentle music over the sounds of the acid seas.

Eliminating Karter had been . . . regrettable. Still, he should have known better than to fall into such an obvious trap. Now he was gone, and his communication device would have been destroyed in the process, leaving Hero Factory with no clues to follow.

At least, that is what he believed . . . but was it true? He wondered.

Stormer and his team were nothing if not resourceful. They might find a way to trace the original transmission back to its source. This temporary base would need to be abandoned. He took comfort in the fact that it was time to move operations into the heart of the galaxy, anyway.

Naturally, he and his colleagues had not been seeking a confrontation with Hero Factory — at least, not this soon. But it was only a matter of time before their moves caught the attention of Makuro or one of his robots. The conspirators were prepared to do what was necessary in that event.

Von Nebula, Black Phantom, Aldous Witch,

and others had tried to ruin Hero Factory—but his team would succeed. As Karter had pointed out, they had money, fleets of ships, not to mention influence on a hundred worlds. They controlled events while remaining hidden in the shadows themselves.

Hero Factory, by contrast, was right out there in public. Everyone knew who they were and where they were. They might as well have painted a big target in the middle of Makuhero City.

Soon, the time would come when he would send out the signal that would spell the beginning of the end for Stormer, Bulk, and the rest. All across the galaxy, his operatives would shed their disguises and put the final plan into action. Once begun, this could not be stopped—and its end would be the destruction of everyone who had ever called themselves "Hero."

Stormer stood at a viewport, staring out into space.

"You're thinking about him again, aren't you?" Breez asked.

Stormer nodded. More and more, his thoughts had been going back to the other Preston Stormer, the one who suffered so for his heroism. *Could I have gone through what he went through?* he wondered. *Would I have had the strength to fight again, after so many years?*

"It's funny, but I keep thinking of Von Nebula," said Breez. "Just like in our universe, he tried to be more than anyone else — only there, he ended up much less."

That was true, Stormer thought. *If our Von Nebula knew what had happened to his twin, would it make any difference? Or would he stay on the same dark path he's on now?*

"Something else that struck me," she continued. "There was no Breez there."

"Makuro got stopped before he could build you," said Stormer. "But I am sure you will be coming to life there any day now."

"Maybe," Breez said. "If so, I hope she will be

happy there. I hope she will have the same kinds of teammates I have."

Stormer didn't reply. He was thinking about another kind of team, the conspirators who had used Karter and who still threatened Hero Factory. They were as elusive as smoke, so far: impossible to see or touch. But he could feel them closing in, the way one could feel night coming or a storm about to break.

In that other world, they got caught unprepared, Stormer said to himself. *They never saw Von Ness's betrayal coming and they lost everything. I won't—I* can't—*let that happen here.*

Long after Breez left, he continued to stare out at the stars. Somewhere, in another universe, another Stormer was probably looking at the same constellations. In some strange way, that was a comfort.

Good luck, Preston, he thought. *Good luck to both of us.*